Copyright © 2003 by Nord-Süd Verlag AG, Gossau Zürich, Switzerland
First published in Switzerland under the title *Toddel, der mutigste Hase der Welt*.
English translation copyright © 2003 by North-South Books Inc., New York

First published in the United States, Great Britain, Canada, Australia,
and New Zealand in 2003 by North-South Books, an imprint
of Nord-Süd Verlag AG, Gossau Zürich, Switzerland.

Distributed in the United States by North-South Books Inc., New York.

Library of Congress Cataloging-in-Publication Data is available.
A CIP catalogue record for this book is available from The British Library.

ISBN 0-7358-1811-8 (trade edition)
1 3 5 7 9 HC 10 8 6 4 2
ISBN 0-7358-1812-6 (library edition)
1 3 5 7 9 LE 10 8 6 4 2
Printed in Belgium

For more information about our books, and the authors and artists
who create them, visit our web site: www.northsouth.com

Timid Timmy

By Andreas Dierssen

Illustrated by Felix Scheinberger

Translated by Marianne Martens

North-South Books

New York / London

Timmy was a very timid little hare, but he longed to be brave like his friend Rocket.

Rocket was fearless. He would leap over water-filled ditches in a single bound, skip through a herd of cows, tease wild boars. And he wasn't even afraid to cross the deep, dark forest alone.

When Timmy and Rocket went to the pond, Rocket would always dare Timmy to jump in. "Come on!" he would call. "Last one in is a chicken!"

One time Timmy decided to try. He stood at the edge of the boulder looking way down into the deep water below. His heart pounded. He closed his eyes, clenched his paws, and then . . . and then . . . and then he chickened out.

Rocket was so daring he'd even steal carrots from the farmer's garden in broad daylight! Timmy wouldn't do that in his wildest dreams.

Timmy told his mother all about
Rocket. "He is the bravest hare in the
world," he said. Then he sighed sadly.
"I'm just a big coward."

"Rocket does seem to be very bold
and daring," Mother said. "But being
fearless doesn't mean you are brave,
and I think you are much braver than
you know."

He would never be as brave as Rocket. Timmy
was sure of that. No matter what his mother said.
He would always be a coward—his whole life.

One day Timmy found a big pile
of carrots just outside the family burrow.
Timmy was hungry and he loved carrots,
so he took a tiny bite. Then another . . .
and another . . . and another . . . and
before he knew it, he had eaten the
whole pile.

That evening, Mother Hare was angry. "Who ate all the carrots?" she asked. No one said a word. Suddenly Timmy's tummy hurt.

"So, who did it?" demanded Mother.

Timmy's nose started twitching, and he couldn't look his mother in the eye.

Timmy couldn't get to sleep that night. He kept thinking about those carrots and how upset his mother had been. It was all his fault. Finally he couldn't stand it any longer. He hopped out of bed and went to find his mother.

"Can't you sleep, Timmy?" Mother Hare asked.

Timmy hung his head. "It was me, Mother," he said. "I ate the carrots. And, and, and—I'm sorry."

Mother Hare didn't say anything for a long time. Finally Timmy asked, "Are you mad at me?"

"No, Timmy," said Mother Hare. "Well, maybe just a little bit. But I'm proud of you. It takes courage to tell the truth, and you were brave to confess. In fact, tonight I think *you* are the bravest hare in the world!"

Timmy glowed with pride. He still wasn't bold and daring and fearless like Rocket, but he *was* truly brave.